ANA IS TRYING TO BE A GOOD SPORT.

Ana braced herself at the starting block. Clarisse was three girls down the line. This time, when the whistle blew, Ana raced into the lead. The first hurdle came up so fast, Ana was surprised. No time to think. She flew over it — and over all the ones after that, feeling her heart pound in her ears as she landed, sneakers thudding in the dirt without stumbling or slowing. She heard footsteps behind her, and poured it on. *It's magic*, Ana thought. Just when she thought all her energy was gone, she found more. Coach Arlen was clapping her hands as Ana crossed the line, three whole steps in front of Clarisse.

"Those were the best hurdles you've ever run, Ana!" Coach Arlen jogged alongside her as Ana cooled down. She slapped Ana on the back. "You're improving mighty fast."

Coach Arlen shouted back to Clarisse, "Better work harder, Clarisse. Ana's the one to beat now."

Great, Ana thought. *Now Coach Arlen has given Clarisse even more reason to hate me.*

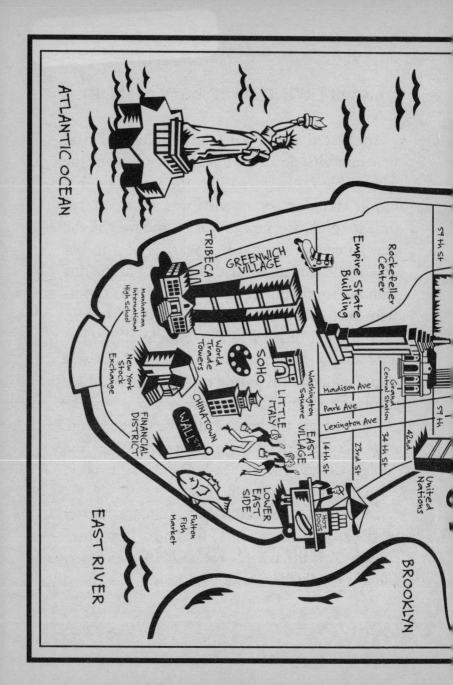

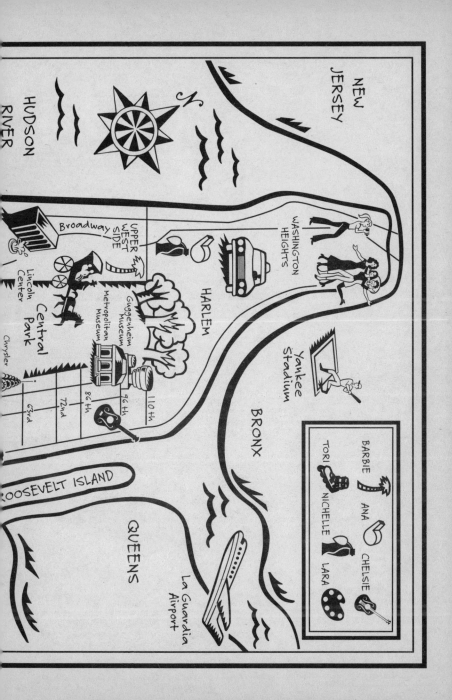

#3

Pushing

the Limits

By Melanie Stewart

A GOLD KEY PAPERBACK
Golden Books Publishing Company, Inc.
New York

A GOLD KEY Paperback Original

Golden Books Publishing Company, Inc.
888 Seventh Avenue
New York, NY 10106

Cover photography by Graham Kuhn.

Interior art by Amy Bryant.

ISBN: 0-307-23452-5

First Gold Key paperback printing June 1999

10 9 8 7 6 5 4 3 2

Printed in the U.S.A.

GENERATI✱N GIRL™

Pushing
the Limits

Chapter 1

"Pardon Me, Is This Your Sandal?"

Eatz was packed to the rafters with International High School students trying to get a burger, and Ana Suarez fought her way through the after-school crowd. Eatz was the girls' favorite hangout, a cool little diner about one block from the school. The food wasn't great, but the prices were cheap and the owner didn't mind the place being mobbed by I. H. students after school.

I just have to get a bigger locker for all my gear, Ana thought for the twelfth time that day. Finally she spotted Barbie Roberts, waving her hand

1

frantically from a booth all the way at the back. Thank goodness! Ana balanced her history books on top of her gym bag and craned her head to see. Nichelle Williams was in the booth, too, reading a fashion magazine and putting on purple lipstick.

Ana laughed. She'd been so worried at first that she wouldn't fit in at International High. But then she'd met Barbie, Nichelle, and their cool group of friends and realized her fears were groundless. Her new friends came from all over — Barbie was from California, Lara and Chelsie were from Europe, pretty African American Nichelle was from Harlem, and Tori was from Australia. They'd made Ana feel warm and appreciated from the moment she'd met them.

Suddenly, Ana felt a tremendous shove right against her elbow. Her books went flying through the air, and clothing from her half-open gym bag scattered everywhere. She looked around and saw a skateboarder tearing through the crowd for the open front door. *He must have bumped me*, thought Ana, looking down at her stuff scattered all over the floor. *What a creep!*

Even worse, she heard a wave of giggles from the table right in front of her. It was Clarisse Stephenson and her whole group of friends, staring at Ana and laughing. Ana sighed inside. Clarisse was on the track team with Ana, and was a strong runner. Ana wanted to like her, for the good of the team. But Clarisse was extremely competitive, and Ana wasn't about to lose a race just to keep Clarisse happy. Not when her chances for a college scholarship rode on it.

"Everything okay down there, An-n-a?" Clarisse said in a fake sweet voice, twisting her straight red hair around her hairbrush. Clarisse's friends collapsed in giggles again. Cheeks burning with embarrassment, Ana knelt down and gathered up her wet towel and bathing suit from the floor. She wasn't going to give Clarisse the satisfaction of answering her.

"Those skateboarder guys can be such jerks," a friendly voice said, right behind Ana. "They just don't care who they run over." Ana looked up to see who had spoken. A tall, brown-haired boy with blue eyes stood over her. "Let me help you with that." He knelt down and reached for her waterproof sandals, which had slid under the edge of the counter.

"Oh, that's okay," Ana said hurriedly. "I can handle it. I don't want you to lose your place in line."

"Oh, it's no problem. My friend's holding my spot." He handed her the sandals as she shouldered the gym bag, and she tucked one of them under her arm. "I've seen you at I. H. My name's Blaine Gordon." He stuck his hand out for Ana to shake.

Ana extended a hand, too, and then, realizing it still had a sandal in it, she laughed. "I'm Ana. Ana Suarez."

Blaine took the sandal from her and put it in her gym bag. They both laughed. Another boy shouted from the head of the line, "Hey, Blaine, we're up. Get up here and order!"

"Got to run, Ana. But I'll see you at school!" Blaine walked through the crowd and disappeared, heading for the cashier. Clarisse and her friends had stopped laughing, Ana realized.

Suddenly she felt better. Maybe I. H. wouldn't be so bad after all.

When she finally reached her friends, Ana threw herself down into the orange plastic booth with a melodramatic sigh. Barbie and Nichelle looked up. "So who's the major hunk?" Nichelle asked with a big smile.

"Who?" Ana said blankly, taking a big sip from her water bottle.

"The guy who helped you with your bag? Hello, Earth to Ana!" Nichelle dropped her fashion magazine and threw her hands up in frustration. Barbie laughed out loud and pushed a bowl of green salad over to Ana.

"I ordered this for you, just like you asked," Barbie said. "I don't know how you manage to eat such healthy food, Ana."

"Me either," said Nichelle. "I couldn't live without my french fries."

"Just trying to stay in training for the Central Park Triathlon, guys," Ana said. "I've got to be able to run, swim, and bike. But as soon as it's over, the first thing I'm doing is eating a big ice-cream sundae."

"Yeah, and I'll be filming you at the finish line," Barbie said. Barbie loved her new video camera, a gift from her parents. She filmed her friends every chance she got.

"So who was the guy?" Nichelle asked for the second time. "Not half bad, Ana," she said, nudging Ana in the ribs.

"Oh, stop it, Nichelle. All he did was pick up my sandals! He said his name was Blaine."

"Blaine? As in Blaine Gordon?" Barbie asked. "Isn't he running for student body president?"

"Looks like you'll have a chance to ask him yourself," Nichelle said in a very loud whisper. "Here he comes now!"

"Oh, very funny, Nichelle," Ana said, rolling her eyes.

Then Blaine tapped her on the shoulder. "Hi, Ana," Blaine said. "I forgot to give you this." He handed her her history textbook.

"Thanks," Ana said shyly. "Uh, these are my friends, Nichelle and Barbie."

"Nice to meet you," Blaine said politely, keeping his eyes on Ana. "Would you," he said awkwardly, "I mean . . . I know you're in my history class." Blaine started again. "Would you like to study together sometime? I mean all of us," he said suddenly, including Nichelle and Barbie in his look.

Ana sat with her mouth open. Nichelle jumped right in before she could close it. "Sure!" Nichelle sang out. "Ana would love to."

"Great!" Blaine said, "I'll see you tomorrow after class, guys." Blaine walked away quickly, shouldering his backpack.

"Nichelle," Ana shrieked. "I can't believe you did that!"

"Ooooh," Nichelle said, "it was worth it." She smiled broadly and pointed across the room. "Will you look at that?"

Ana looked in the direction Nichelle pointed. "So, it's Clarisse. So what?"

"Does she look happy?" Nichelle asked. Then she answered her own question. "No, she does not. And why doesn't she look happy? Because she had her eye on Blaine, and he" — Nichelle pointed at Ana dramatically — "had his eye on you!"

Ana looked over at Clarisse. It was true,

Clarisse did look pretty mad! *Great, one more reason for her not to like me.*

Barbie said, "Don't worry about Clarisse. Maybe she's jealous, but she'll get over it in no time."

"I hope so," Ana said, looking at her watch. "I'd better hurry. I'm going to miss my bus, and I told Mama I'd be home early today." Ana gulped down the last few bites of her salad as fast as she could.

"Tell you what," Barbie said, "I'll walk you to the bus stop."

"It's a little hike," said Ana.

"That's okay. It's more fun for me because you know the city better than I do."

It was true, Ana thought. She knew New York better than anywhere, because she'd never lived anywhere else. Her parents left Mexico before she was born to find better work in New York. But for all that Mama and Papa talked about Mexico as home, Ana only remembered a few things from her visits there as a little kid. Her *abuela* — grandma — lifting her up to pick a pink flower, and an adobe house made of red mud. *I'm a New York girl*, Ana thought, looking around at the skyscrapers and taxis. *This is home for me.*

Pushing the Limits

It was always fun walking with Barbie. She had a great eye for detail, and because she was new to the city, she noticed things and people that Ana would have missed just because she saw them every day: Old men playing chess in the park and yelling at each other because they were going deaf; and art students, one with pink hair and one with purple hair, painting a mural of dolphins and the ocean on the side of a store. Ana and Barbie turned a corner by a florist's shop, dodging a bike messenger who raced by.

"Ana, look at that darling little dog," Barbie said. The fluffy white poodle trotted along the sidewalk like she ruled the world, pink bows in her hair. The girls stopped to pet her and asked the girl walking her what the dog's name was.

"Princess," the dog walker said, "and can you believe I get paid a hundred dollars a week to walk her?"

"Wow, a hundred dollars a week," Barbie marveled. "Can you believe that, Ana?"

Ana couldn't. *A hundred dollars a week just to walk a dog*, she thought.

"Could I walk a dog, too?" Ana asked quickly.

"I mean, do you ever need extra dog walkers?" A hundred dollars would buy a great pair of running shoes, and Ana was saving up for a new racing bike, too. She also had her eye on a beautiful orchid for Mama.

The young woman laughed. "Sorry, honey. It's just me, and I need all the business I can get."

Barbie was petting Princess and laughing at her little rhinestone collar. Ana smiled at her friend, who always knew how to cheer Ana up. It was hard to worry about anything with Barbie around. Even Clarisse!

"Oh, Barbie, there's my bus!" Ana said quickly, watching the bus barrel down the street toward them.

"Great! I'll see you tomorrow morning before class." Ana waved good-bye from the door of the bus, and again from the window. Barbie waved back, pretending to crank an imaginary movie camera filming Ana going away down the street.

Chapter 2

The Suarez Family

Ana walked home from the bus stop, carefully avoiding a pile of broken glass by the curb. It was a very different neighborhood from the trendy stores and restaurants around I. H. There was some graffiti on the walls of the buildings, and the one small corner grocery store had bars on the windows. But Ana saw the bright flowers of Mrs. Jimenez's window boxes nodding in the breeze above the store, and heard salsa music playing. Three little girls were skipping rope in time with the music, and Ana wanted to stop to watch them, but she

11

was almost late as it was. She'd told Mama she would stop to get more cilantro and onions from the corner store.

Ana pushed open the glass door of the little grocery, and the bells tinkled above to announce her. The store smelled like oranges and cigars. Mrs. Jimenez, who ran the store with her son, looked up and smiled when she saw Ana. Mrs. Jimenez had grown up in the same village in Mexico as Ana's mother, and she loved Ana like a daughter.

"Ana, you look so good!" Mrs. Jimenez opened her arms wide and spoke in Spanish. She gave Ana a crushing hug as she continued. "But I think you need to eat more. Exercise, exercise is all you do! Do you like your new school?"

"Yes, I do," Ana answered in Spanish. "I like my new friends. Do you have fresh cilantro today? Oh, and Mama wants onions, too."

"Only the best for your mama. Did I ever tell you, when your mama and I were girls . . ." Mrs. Jimenez rattled on without even stopping to breathe, but while she talked, she was efficiently bustling around the tiny store, picking out the best onions for Ana, and the freshest cilantro. "You give these to your mother and tell her I am making flan on Sunday and she should come over!"

"Yes, Mrs. Jimenez," Ana said again in Spanish. Despite being in New York for more than ten years, Mrs. Jimenez only spoke a few words of English. Whenever Ana asked her about it, she would say, "Why speak English? All of us here in the neighborhood speak Spanish, anyway! So why bother?"

And in this neighborhood, Ana thought, Mrs. Jimenez was right. Everyone spoke Spanish here whether they were from Mexico, from the Dominican Republic, from Puerto Rico, or from Cuba . . . always Spanish. It was their own little world hidden inside of New York. Ana laughed at the idea. It was as if she were crossing the border every day, going from the all-Spanish world of her family to the all-English world of I. H.

Ana groaned as she entered her apartment building, thinking of her heavy books, her gym bag, and the groceries she had to lug upstairs.

Well, Ana thought, *I get more exercise in a third-floor walk-up.* Ana opened the front door with a key, and pushed it open. The hallway was narrow, with a cracked linoleum floor, and the stairs creaked as she walked up the three flights. Her papa's construction business had been doing really well the past three years, and every year he tried to get Mama to agree to move to a better neighborhood. They'd been talking about it again yesterday, Ana remembered.

Ana's papa had said, "I saw a whole floor of a nice brownstone for rent in a better neighborhood. Closer to Ana's school and everything, Marta. We're well off now, we can live better."

Ana's mama had said, "Better? What is better about moving away from all my friends? So we can go live somewhere where nobody speaks Spanish?"

Ana's papa had just rolled his eyes and thrown his hands in the air. Mama still missed Mexico, particularly in the winter. And she still spoke Spanish more than English, even outside the house. Papa's English was perfect because he needed it to run the business. He wanted Mama to practice her English with Ana and Rosa, Ana's little sister, by speaking it at home. But Mama didn't want to. And when Mama didn't want to do something, she just didn't!

Ana wouldn't have minded moving to a nicer neighborhood, closer to her new friends, but she did see Mama's point. Mama had a million friends here. And, as Mrs. Jimenez said, she didn't need to speak perfect English. In a new neighborhood, Mama would be a stranger who didn't always feel like she belonged. *Kind of like me at International High!*

As Ana opened the door and walked in, Rosa tackled her at the knees. Rosa was four and wanted to be just like Ana, right down to her hair, which she wore in two long, dark ponytails.

"Pick me up, Ana!" Rosa shrieked. "Pick me up!" Ana dropped her gym bag by the door and swung Rosa up onto her shoulders, laughing. She carried Rosa (and the paper bag full of onions and cilantro) into the kitchen, calling for Mama.

The kitchen smelled delicious! Mama was already frying *chorizo* — delicious spicy sausage — in a heavy cast-iron frying pan on the stove. A pot of black beans was simmering next to it. The kitchen was tiny, with only two cramped counters, no windows, and an old stove. There was barely room for the three of them, even with Ana carrying Rosa. Papa had painted the kitchen a cheerful, warm shade of yellow, and Mama had filled every available surface with vases of fresh flowers and plants. It was almost like a garden, Ana thought. The radio played Mexican dance music from the shelf above the sink, and Mama swayed in time to it as she cooked, occasionally breaking into a little dance step.

Mama kissed both girls without putting down her spatula. "Both of my beautiful girls home to help me," she said. Rosa screamed with happiness, right in Ana's ear.

"Don't scream in my ear!" Ana said to Rosa, lowering her to the floor with a *thump*. Rosa looked up, crossed her eyes, and stuck out her tongue.

"Can I scream in your nose?" Rosa asked, giggling. Ana just rolled her eyes. *Little sisters!*

Mama poked Ana in the back with a wooden spoon. "Can you chop the onions and make the rice, Ana? Your father will be home soon."

Ana pulled out the heavy wooden cutting board and a kitchen knife and began chopping the onions, squinting her eyes so they wouldn't water from the sharp onion smell. She'd never be as good of a cook as her mother. She was always too busy with school and sports to concentrate on cooking. She chopped onions slowly and carefully, but the pieces still came out big and awkward, not small and neat like Mama's. Ana filled a pot with water for the rice, moving the beans to the back burner. A little bit of bean juice slopped over the side and onto the stove. *Oh well*, Ana thought, *at least I'm good at sports*.

From the kitchen, Ana heard the front door slam and then a deep bear-like growl. Rosa jumped up as their father swept into the room.

Papa was still wearing his tool belt, and his hard hat was tucked under his arm. He was a heavyset man, with big hands that were rough from hard work, and black eyes that sparkled with fun. He roared like a bear and chased little Rosa, who laughed and ran away.

Mama turned from the stove. "José, don't you get Rosa's dress dirty. I do enough laundry!" So

17

Papa came and gave Mama a bear hug instead, holding his hands up in the air carefully so he wouldn't touch her dress. Now the kitchen was way too crowded!

"And there's my Ana!" Papa said, giving her a big hug. "How's my sports star?" *Estrellita* — little star — had been Papa's nickname for Ana when she was Rosa's age.

"Where's my handsome son?" Papa asked, pretending to peek around doors and windows.

"I'm watching football," Juan called from the living room. Juan was Ana's older brother and he'd just turned eighteen in May. That was the day he'd announced to the family that he wasn't going straight to college. He'd signed up with the navy instead. Mama had cried and Papa had yelled, but gradually they'd gotten used to the idea. Juan had done well in basic training. Ana thought he looked like a grown man in his uniform, even if he was still her annoying older brother.

Mama and Papa started discussing how their day had been so Ana took the opportunity to sit with Juan for a little while. Juan was sitting on the sofa watching TV when Ana joined him.

Pushing the Limits

"Hey, Juan, how are you doing? I am so beat!" Ana slumped tiredly on the sofa next to her brother. "My new school is so far away, I live on the bus and the subway."

Juan studied her. Then he laughed, "Do you know, you look just like Mama when you're tired?"

"You take that back!" Ana said, giggling, and the two of them wrestled on the couch, laughing and hitting each other with pillows. Rosa ran in to join them, and piled in on top of the pair, yelling that dinner was ready.

The whole family ate at the round table at the other end of the living room. Mama was smiling, serving out the food. Papa had Rosa sitting on his knee. And Juan in his navy uniform, looking so grown up but eating as fast as ever. Ana wondered if Clarisse was eating in a big dining room, with butlers and fancy silver candlesticks and fine china. She looked around her family's crowded, noisy apartment, full of talk and laughter and good food, and thought that for once she was happy with things just the way they were.

"Hey, guess what?" Juan said. "I found out where my first posting is!"

"Where, Juan?" Mama asked. "Not too far away?"

"I'll give you a clue." Juan ran into the other room. He came back wearing a necklace of plastic flowers! *"Aloha, Mamacita!"*

"Hawaii." Ana clapped her hands. "Can we visit you right away? Like, next week?"

Juan gave Rosa the plastic flowers, which she wore all through dinner. Ana was thrilled for Juan. He gave her his address at the base so she could write him.

"I'll be leaving in two weeks, so send me pictures of you winning the triathlon," he said. Ana promised that she would. Mama would be sad that Juan was so far away, Ana knew, but the whole family was proud of him.

Ana went to her bedroom after dinner, desperately wanting to go to sleep. Her days were so packed and exhausting, and being at a brand-new school added to the stress. But her homework still waited. Her fat, black cat Gordo was snoozing right on top of her desk, on the open pages of her history book.

"Gordo, you silly cat! I can't read with you lying there." Ana picked Gordo up and dumped him onto the floor, where he stretched his front and back paws lazily before jumping up to Ana's bed. Ana cranked through her homework, focusing extra hard on history. Even if Nichelle was wrong, Ana still wanted to impress Blaine, the cute boy she'd met at Eatz. It couldn't hurt, anyway.

She set her alarm for 5:00 A.M. before she went to bed. If she got to school early, she'd have the track all to herself before school started, and she could still meet Barbie and Nichelle before class. Gordo settled down on her pillow, purring in Ana's ear as she fell asleep.

Chapter 3

The Note Behind the Tile

Ana stepped off the subway at 6:15 A.M. with a spring in her step. She held her breath. Boy, did these tunnels reek! She ran up the stairs to get to the fresh air. She loved being up early! The city was never totally quiet, but this early you could hear birds singing.

She thought of her papa, running construction sites all day. He worked harder running his construction business than any lawyer or accountant in a fancy office. Ana munched on a sports bar as she walked, and dropped the wrapper in a trash can. Mama wanted her to eat a traditional breakfast, but Ana liked her sports bars and juice instead. Extra vitamins in much less time.

Ana slid her student ID into the computerized lock of the side door, and the door clicked open. Most of the students didn't get these special access cards, but members of the sports teams needed them so that they could get into the school to practice at weird hours. Ana loved being able to come and go as she pleased.

The school was super modern, with all the latest technology. Yet the stupidest stuff was always breaking down. One moment the water fountains would squirt you right in the face, the next they would just trickle. Sometimes the elevators worked, sometimes they didn't.

On the way to her locker on the fifth floor, Ana checked under the loose floor tile for a note. After Tori had discovered the tile by accident, it had become a message center for all her friends. Ana saw a folded note with her name on it, written in fancy script on creamy linen stationery. Barbie had pink stationery, so it wasn't from her. And Nichelle's stationery was always purple, her favorite color. *So who else would be writing her?* Ana wondered.

23

Ana opened the note. It was from Chelsie. Chelsie Peterson was maybe the most gifted writer of all her friends. She wrote so well, in fact, that Mr. Toussaint, the adviser to the *Generation Beat*, the school newspaper and web site, had recently promoted her to assistant managing editor, a really prestigious job for a lowly sophomore. Ana always thought of Chelsie as a lovable flake. She was British, which gave her a cool accent, but she was, personally, really disorganized. She was always dropping papers everywhere, usually full of poetry and song lyrics. Even the note Ana now held had a big orange juice stain on the beautiful linen paper. The note read:

Dear Ana,
Hello! Pardon the giant orange juice stain on the note, but I've been up since 5 A.M. editing some articles for the paper, and I'm eating breakfast as I write.
I've got a special favor to ask. Mr. Toussaint asked me yesterday if I had any ideas about how to improve our coverage of girls' sports. I immediately thought

of you. I know you're training for the Central Park Triathlon and that you're the only I. H. student entered. Could you — would you — write an article about your experiences? I'll feature it on the sports page. It would be great for the cause of girls' sports and it would also solve a major problem for me. I'll meet you for lunch today, so you can tell me, "Yes!" (If you say no, I'm going to cover my ears and hum so I can't hear it.) So do say yes.

Ta,
Chelsie

Ana laughed. Chelsie managed to sound both British and ditzy in her note. But Ana thought writing the article sounded kind of cool, if she could write it after the triathlon was over. She dashed off a quick note on a piece of notebook paper, accepting Chelsie's lunch invitation.

Ana walked through the underground tunnel to the gym, then up the stairs and through the outside doors onto the track. The air was crisp and clear. Ana pulled on her lucky blue T-shirt over her track gear. It was almost worn through in spots, but she wasn't giving it up until it fell apart. It had been Juan's shirt once. He had worn it on the day he had hit a home run for his high school baseball team, winning the city championship. Maybe it would be lucky for Ana, too.

Ana did her stretches carefully, making sure every muscle was warmed up and ready. Her new cross-training shoes had been a birthday present, and she loved how they still felt springy and new. She started jogging slowly, and then worked up to a steady pace. The bleachers flew by. Her heart beat steadily, and Ana felt like she could run forever. None of her worries — money, school, her family — could touch her when she ran.

She slowed her pace after six miles, jogging another lap to cool down. Then she ran into the locker room for a quick shower, changing into her bathing suit. Ana tucked her long dark hair under a bathing cap and slipped on her waterproof sandals. She smiled, thinking of Blaine handing over her sandals at Eatz yesterday.

Ana draped her white towel over the railing and slipped into the water. She still couldn't believe they had a real Olympic-size pool right at school. She appreciated this more than anything.

Pushing the Limits

She'd been a star swimmer at her old school, but the pool there wasn't half as nice as I. H.'s. When she'd transferred to I. H., the swim coach, Sonya Kirov, had introduced himself and urged her to come out for the swim team in the spring. Coach Kirov used to coach Olympic athletes in Russia, so Ana was extremely flattered that he would take an interest in her. But Ana didn't have to wait for spring to get involved in school sports. Coach Arlen, the girls' track team coach, had convinced her to go out for the hurdles and distance races for the track team's fall season. Even as busy as Ana was with track practice, she kept swimming, too. Coach Kirov recorded her swimming times every week, and gave her a tough time if she missed even a single day of swimming.

It was great to have a whole lane to herself. She watched the giant clock on the wall to judge her starting time down to the second, and then kicked off from the wall. Ana swam forty laps, stroking steadily. She surfaced at the far end of the pool to see Nichelle sitting there on the bleachers, reading a textbook and scribbling in a notebook.

Nichelle looked up and clapped. "Ana, you are a machine! I knew you'd be here, so I came in to meet you."

"Are you going to swim, too?" Ana asked.

"Just a few laps," Nichelle said. "Now that I've finished my math homework, anyway." Nichelle slammed her math textbook shut.

"Ms. Newton sure piles it on, doesn't she?" Ana said. "It's like she thinks we have nothing else to do but her one class."

Nichelle joined Ana in the pool, pulling on big purple goggles. "Have to keep my eyes from getting red," Nichelle joked. "You don't see Naomi Campbell with red eyes!" Nichelle wanted to be a model. "But a smart model," Nichelle always said. "A model who knows what's up."

The two girls worked through a few more laps, and then changed and raced to class. Nichelle had biology first period, and Ana had English. Ana had just enough time to drop off her gym bag in her locker and grab her books. She dashed into class thirty seconds before the bell rang. Barbie waved from her desk, which was next to Ana's, and started to speak, but the bell cut off her words.

Pushing the Limits

"Did you get Chelsie's note?" Barbie whispered. Barbie also worked on the school newspaper, the *Generation Beat,* and she was always looking for stories. Barbie loved talking to everybody. She said that talking with other people made her a better actress. It was a way for her to learn how different people spoke and moved.

"Yes, I'm meeting her for lunch," Ana whispered back. She thought it was great that Barbie knew what she wanted to do when she grew up. Ana knew she had to get a college scholarship. She wasn't sure yet what she would study when she got to college. Maybe law. Or medicine. Something professional. She just hadn't decided.

Mr. Toussaint cut off their conversation by knocking lightly on Ana's desk with one knuckle. "Perhaps *you* know what Romeo meant in that last line," he said with a devilish grin. He knew perfectly well she had no idea.

Barbie rolled her eyes in apology to Ana. Mr. Toussaint was the most popular teacher in school, and usually he was pretty easygoing. If you did the readings, he was actually pretty funny. But Ana had forgotten to finish reading the play this morning. She stared at the line and answered as best she could, crossing her fingers in hopes that he wouldn't notice. It was good enough, apparently, because he went on to someone else.

International High was a whole new world for Ana. She had always gotten straight A's at the regular public school. But here at I. H., the competition was much tougher. The teachers expected so much more. Sometimes it was kind of a strain.

Luckily, the morning flew by. Barbie got called on in French, but she got through it. "I know all the right words in French," Barbie moaned to Ana as they split up to go to their third-period classes, "but my accent still sounds so Californian! I'm going to listen to the language tapes again tonight."

Their friend Lara Morelli-Strauss laughed. Lara said to Barbie, "Don't worry, *chérie*, I will help you." Lara was half German and half Italian, but she had lived in Paris most of her life, so she spoke English with an adorable French accent. "Hold your mouth just so when you speak."

"You have to learn to speak French, Barbie. You'd look so good in a beret!" Nichelle had sneaked up behind them. "*Bonjour* and all that! Ana, have you seen Blaine yet?"

A steady stream of people were pushing by them on their way to class. Clarisse and her group of girls giggled meanly as they passed by Ana. Or at least Ana thought they sounded mean. Maybe she was just being paranoid.

It was just bad luck that Clarisse's last name was Stephenson. It meant her locker was right next to Ana's. Clarisse threw her locker door open with a bang. Why couldn't her last name have started with a Z, Ana wondered, or an A? Anywhere else but right next to Ana's. Clarisse stood there, brushing out her red hair and putting on lip gloss in the mirror she had put inside her locker door on the first day of class. Ana could stand her primping and hogging all the space. She was used to that. But Clarisse was so obviously eavesdropping on what Nichelle was saying.

"No, you know I don't have history until fifth period," Ana answered Nichelle. "Does my hair look okay?" Ana was only half joking. It's not like she cared what Blaine thought or anything. After all, she had just met him the other day. But she had worn her favorite earrings and blue blouse, anyway. "I probably won't see Blaine then, anyway."

"Sure you will," Nichelle said loudly, leaning forward and winking. Clearly she'd noticed Clarisse listening, too. "Blaine is so into you."

Lara said, "*Oui!* He looks for you all morning."

Clarisse slammed shut her locker door so hard that they all heard the mirror rattle in its frame. Then she stalked off down the hallway.

"That'll teach her to eavesdrop," Nichelle said. She imitated Clarisse's walk for a few steps. "That girl thinks she's all that!"

Ana laughed. Nichelle was wonderful at imitating people. Barbie shook her head despairingly at both of them. "Oh sure, and I suppose we can say it was Clarisse's fault when we're sent to detention for being late to class." With that, the four girls scattered down the hallway in different directions.

Ana shouted back over her shoulder to Barbie

and Nichelle. "I'll meet you guys for lunch in the cafeteria." Even though I. H.'s cafeteria was brand-new, the cafeteria food was mysteriously the same as any other school: Bad! Mystery meat in glue sauce. But Mrs. Simmons, I. H.'s principal, had promised it would be getting better soon. *It couldn't get any worse*, Ana thought. *When you hit the bottom, there's nowhere to go but up.* Technically, the girls could leave school for lunch. But with only forty minutes for lunch, they often didn't have the time.

Barbie called back, "Okay! See you there," before she disappeared around the corner.

Ana went off to art class with a sigh of relief. Art class was restful in comparison to her other classes. Ana was happy for the chance to sketch in peace. Even Tori, the wild Australian girl, liked Mrs. Glottel, the art teacher. She swept into the room dramatically and flicked on the stereo. Classical music poured out.

Ana quickly finished her assigned sketch of an iris in a vase, and started sketching Mr. Toussaint's face from memory on a piece of scrap paper.

Tori tapped her shoulder. "That's a good

drawin' you got there! You should show 'im." Her voice was remarkably quiet for once. Tori lived her life at full throttle, skating everywhere she went. Her blond hair crackled with life even when she tied it in her trademark ponytails.

"I like yours, too, Tori," Ana said, glancing over her shoulder. Tori's drawing of the flower was very modern and abstract. Broad swatches of bright violet and neon green crossed over the charcoal outlines of the drawing without regard to the boundaries. "It's really different."

"That's me. Ms. Different!"

Ana's parents drove her nuts sometimes, but she couldn't imagine living across the world from her family.

"How's your aunt?" Ana asked. Tori's family had sent her to live in New York with her elderly aunt, Tessa, who turned out to be a famous artist.

"You'll never believe it! I got Aunt Tessa up on in-line skates last week! We went skating in Central Park. You should come with us next time."

"I wish I could." Ana loved to skate, even though she didn't own her own pair of in-line skates. But Tori had a ton of extra pairs, and she and Ana wore the same shoe size — at least if Ana wore extrathick socks. "But until the triathlon is done, I officially have no life! Run, swim, bike, and that's it."

The bell rang for lunch. "So do you want to come to lunch? I'm meeting Barbie and Nichelle. And Chelsie, too," Ana said, remembering her lunch meeting plans. "Oh, I forgot, you've got the early lunch schedule."

"Yeah, usually I'd be outta luck, seeing as how I. H. decided to make my lunch in the morning, the lamebrains!" Tori said. "It's bonzer that Lara has early lunch, too, or I'd die of boredom on the spot! But my class was cancelled today, and I want to chat with Chelsie about the web page. Plus, it's better not to eat the garbage they serve all on your own. If you die of food poisoning, who'll call the ambulance?"

Ana laughed as she and Tori made their way down to the cafeteria. Nichelle had staked out a table right in the center of things. She was already eating a fruit salad. Next to her sat Chelsie, grimly prodding her fork into the mystery entrée. Chelsie was wearing a navy blazer and skirt and a white blouse. Ana wondered why she chose outfits like that. It practically looked like a uniform.

"It's worse than airplane food," Chelsie said, looking at her tray. "I don't know how they do it."

"They've bought the worldwide rights to the *Bad Food Cookbook*," Barbie said, carrying a salad and a soda on her tray. "Hi, guys," she said. "How was art?"

"Splendiferous and outstanding, mate," Tori sang out.

Ana grabbed an extra chair from the next table for herself. "Try the salad, Chelsie. It's got a lower mortality rate."

Nichelle guarded the table while the girls waited in line. When they got back, Nichelle jumped up to get ice cream. Barbie went with her.

Ana asked, "So you're assistant managing editor?"

"Yes," Chelsie said, "and it's so much work half the time, I don't know what to do first. Picking the stories and editing them are the fun part. But the deadlines are sending me into a tizzy!" Chelsie's backpack was bulging with papers, and there were big, dark circles under her eyes. "I don't remember when I last got enough sleep."

"So is the fancy outfit your new editor's uniform?" Ana asked teasingly.

Chelsie groaned out loud. "No, Mum went on one of her little fits again. I have to dress like a little prep school victim and be inspected every morning."

"Ick."

"Oh, she'll forget about it in a few weeks. But till then" — Chelsie tugged the sleeve of her blazer — "it's welcome to the world of wool and tweed."

Chelsie took a sip of soda and went on. "So, have you thought about writing the article?"

"I'd love to do it, but I'm super short of time right now. Can I hand it in a few days after the triathlon?"

"No problem. Actually, I feel kind of silly about this. I've been meaning to ask you to write this piece for a long time. I didn't need Mr. Toussaint to tell me."

"You could have just asked me." Ana smiled at Chelsie.

"Yes, but you are so busy, I didn't want to bug you," Chelsie said, gazing down at her mystery meat.

"No, I'm glad to write the article. Really!" Ana reassured her. "It'll be cool. And if you need help organizing *Generation Beat*, I'll be there for you as soon as the triathlon is finished."

Chapter 4

Whispering in the Locker Room

Last period was history class. Ana sat in the front row, so she had to be subtle as she looked over her shoulder to find Blaine in the back row. The last thing she wanted was for Blaine to think she was staring. But from her angle all the way up front, she didn't have much choice!

Finally, Ana pretended to drop her notebook on the floor behind her desk so she could turn around without feeling stupid. She picked the notebook up slowly, but she didn't see him. Some other boy was sitting in Blaine's regular desk in the back row. It was Ivor, the Russian transfer student. That was strange, because he usually sat up in the front row next to Ana. What was going on? As the bell rang, Blaine ran in through the door and piled his books on the empty desk.

"Hi Ana," Blaine said. "I hope you don't mind the switch." He pulled out a pair of glasses and settled them on his face. "I just got glasses, and Ivor said he'd trade desks with me until I get used to wearing them." He smiled at Ana. "Unless you mind."

Her mind went totally blank. *Say something quick, or Blaine's going to think you're a total geek!*

Ana said, "No, I don't mind. Why would I mind?" Mind? She was thrilled. Ivor had just gotten here from Russia, and he didn't speak English very well. Plus Ivor blew his nose all the time in a cloth handkerchief. Major gross. Sitting next to Blaine had to be better than that. Besides, she was beginning to think Nichelle was right. Maybe Blaine did like her.

She checked him out with a sideways look, trying not to get caught. Nope, she hadn't been imagining it. Blaine was pretty cute, even with glasses. Dark, wavy hair and nice, sparkling blue eyes. Things were looking up!

"It might make history more fun," Ana said.

"I live to improve your life, my lady," Blaine said, pretending to bow in his seat.

Ten minutes (or was it ten hours?) into the class, Blaine passed her a note under the edge of her desk. Ana picked up her textbook, holding it at a slight angle to hide the note. She opened it. The note said:

I think I've discovered the cure for insomnia! Think I can sell it and make a million?

Ana smothered a giggle. She flipped the note over and scribbled back on the other side.

You'll be richer than Bill Gates! But we'll still both fail history if we get caught snoring in class. I'll give you a million if you just keep me awake!

History went faster than usual with Blaine sitting next to her. It only seemed to take one eternity, instead of two, anyway. Finally the bell rang. The two of them walked out and down the hallway, and right into Clarisse. *Just when things were going so well*, Ana thought with a sigh.

"Hi, Blaine," Clarisse said in a sugary-sweet voice. She didn't even look at Ana. "You know, you missed my birthday last week. I thought you'd at least *call*."

"Oh," Blaine mumbled. "Happy birthday."

Ana's heart sank. What kind of relationship did Blaine have with Clarisse, anyhow? Did Clarisse have some kind of claim on him? He didn't act like it, but *she* sure did.

Clarisse kept chattering at Blaine, totally ignoring Ana.

Ana knew Clarisse didn't like her, but this was ridiculous. They were on the track team together, after all. It's not like they'd never met. Ana felt like waving her hand in front of Clarisse's face. *Hel-lo! Am I invisible?*

Blaine suddenly interrupted Clarisse and said, "I'm sorry, do you know Ana?"

Clarisse waved her hand dismissively. "Blaine —"

"Yes, she knows me," Ana interrupted. "We're on the track team together!"

"You run track, too?" Blaine asked Ana. "That is so cool." He smiled at her. "No wonder you're in such good shape." He turned back to Clarisse. "Sorry, Clarisse. What were you saying again?"

"Oh, forget it!" Clarisse stomped off down the hall.

"What's her problem?" Blaine stared after her.

"Like she said, forget it," Ana said with a grin.

Blaine looked confused, and then shrugged. "Whatever. Let me just go dump my books in my locker and I'll be right back."

"Great," Ana said. Across the hall, she spotted Nichelle, who flashed her a thumbs-up sign. "I'll meet you right over there by Nichelle in ten minutes," Ana told Blaine.

"Good deal. Back in a flash!"

Ana dashed over to say hi to Nichelle.

"I love seeing Clarisse get ticked off!" Nichelle said with satisfaction. "Now all you have to do is beat her at practice today, and your day will be complete."

"Practice?" Ana wailed in despair. "I forgot about practice!" Ana looked at her watch. Barely enough time if she ran to change right now! But she'd told Blaine she'd wait for him by Nichelle's locker. He'd think Ana had ditched him. She smacked her hand against Nichelle's locker in frustration. "I am such an idiot!"

"I'll tell Blaine you forgot about practice, and you had to run," Nichelle said reassuringly. "He'll understand."

"Tell him I'll talk to him before history tomorrow. I owe you big time, Nichelle."

"And don't you forget it, girl!"

Ana picked up her gym bag and hustled to the locker room. She threw on her workout clothes and her lucky T-shirt from Juan and made it out to the track.

The team was gathered at the starting block. Most of them had on their nice new tracksuits in green and gold, the school colors. But Ana was kind of superstitious about giving up her lucky outfit.

After stretching, they started with sprints. Ana loved them. That quick burst of energy, a cool breeze hitting her face, and then bang! The race was over. But Clarisse was a strong sprinter.

Stronger than Ana. Clarisse beat her two times out of three. But Ana was right on her heels for the third sprint. *A few more weeks, and I might even win one*, Ana thought.

Ana's strength was distance running. Great for the triathlon, but not so great for beating Clarisse. But Ana and Clarisse were about evenly matched in the next event, the hurdles.

She braced herself at the starting block. Clarisse was three girls down the line. This time, when the whistle blew, Ana raced into the lead. The first hurdle came up so fast, Ana was surprised. No time to think. She flew over it — and over all the ones after that, feeling her heart pound in her ears as she landed, sneakers thudding in the dirt without stumbling or slowing. She heard footsteps behind her, and poured it on. *It's magic*, Ana thought. Just when she thought all her energy was gone, she found more. Coach Arlen was clapping her hands as Ana crossed the line, three whole steps in front of Clarisse.

"Those were the best hurdles you've ever run,

Ana!" Coach Arlen jogged alongside her as Ana cooled down. She slapped Ana on the back. "You're improving mighty fast."

Coach Arlen shouted back to Clarisse, "Better work harder, Clarisse. Ana's the one to beat now."

Great, Ana thought. *Now Coach Arlen has given Clarisse even more reason to hate me.*

* * * * * *

After practice, Ana was drying her hair with a towel. When she heard her name, she lifted her head out of the towel. It was Tiffany, a friend of Clarisse's who was also on the team. They were talking on the other side of the gym lockers, but their voices echoed all the way back to where Ana stood.

Tiffany said, "I heard that Blaine has a thing for Ana. Can you believe that? I mean, what does he see in her? I mean, look at her workout clothes! They're practically falling apart."

"Well, you know Blaine," Clarisse said scornfully. "He is such a do-gooder. He's so soft-hearted."

"What's that got to do with it?" Tiffany sounded puzzled.

"Isn't it obvious? He feels sorry for her. You know, help the poor Hispanic girl feel at home with the rich kids! Did you know she lives in Washington Heights? My mom said that her mom came to Parents' Night and could barely speak English! It's just like Blaine to want to help out the less fortunate. It isn't because he likes her or anything! Remember how he worked in that soup kitchen last year."

"Yeah, I guess," Tiffany said.

"It's pitiful to watch. She should have a little more pride than to chase after him like she does!" Clarisse's voice receded as the two girls drifted down the corridor leading out of the locker room.

Ana froze in the doorway, feeling her face go hot and then cold. Was Clarisse right? She had been so stupid. Ana stuffed her sweaty clothes into her bag without folding them. Her throat prickled, and her eyes burned with tears. How could she have thought she would ever fit in at

International High? What was it Blaine had said, "I live to improve your life"? She'd thought he was just kidding around, but maybe what Clarisse had said was true. So what if her mom didn't speak perfect English? Ana wasn't anyone's little charity case. She'd show him!

Ana took the long subway and bus ride back to Washington Heights and walked angrily back to her family's apartment building. She was practicing all the things she should have said to Blaine when he'd taken the desk next to hers in history class. Like "Get lost!" and "This is one little Mexican girl who doesn't need your help, thank you very much!"

She was trying to be tough as she climbed the stairs. But it was hard. She had really liked Blaine, and it made her feel so stupid that she had thought he really liked her, too. Ana had just been starting to feel like she fit in at I. H. Now she felt like she was back at ground zero again.

Her little sister called in Spanish from upstairs, "Ana? Is that you?"

"I'm coming, Rosa." Hastily, Ana wiped the

tears out of her eyes. She couldn't let Rosa see her cry. Or Mama and Papa, either. She was going to be a success at International High. She didn't need Blaine. And who cared about stupid Clarisse? They deserved each other!

Chapter 5

A Cruel Twist of Fate

Ana waited in the hallway to the last possible moment before the bell rang. She wasn't going to give Blaine even the slightest chance to talk to her. She'd been doing this for three days now, and it seemed to be working. He still tried to slip her notes under the desk in Mr. Budge's history class, but she just took them without reading them. She wanted to just crumple them up and drop them on the floor, but she knew that Mr. Budge would catch them. That would be just perfect, having Mr.

Budge read Blaine's stupid notes in front of the whole class. So she just stuck them unopened between the pages of her history book.

She sneaked a glance over at Blaine, who was staring straight ahead, pretending to be interested in Mr. Budge's lecture. As if anyone could be! Blaine had looked so hurt when Ana had walked by him at lunch without speaking. She felt bad then, just for a minute. *What if Clarisse had been wrong?*

I really will fail history at this rate! I'm not listening at all. And when Ana studied at night, all those unopened notes just sat there staring at her. Why did she have to be so stupid to start liking some dumb boy!

The bell rang finally, and Ana escaped without getting called on. Nichelle met her in the hallway right outside.

"Hi, Nichelle," Blaine said from behind Ana.

Great! Now's he's kissing up to Nichelle! I was so right to ignore him.

"Hi, Blaine," Nichelle said cheerfully. "So how are you two doing?"

"Nichelle, can I talk to you for a minute!" Ana grabbed Nichelle by the arm and dragged her down the hallway to her locker.

"Hey, quit pulling on me, girl, have you totally lost your mind?" Nichelle rubbed her arm where Ana had grabbed it. She threw her silver backpack down on the bench by Ana's locker. "You didn't even say good-bye to Blaine."

"I don't care about stupid Blaine!" Ana shouted. Heads snapped around to stare all down the hall.

"What's the matter with you?" Nichelle whispered to Ana, waving her hand to shoo away all the onlookers. "Nothing to see here, folks, move along."

Barbie stuck her head through the crowd. "Does that include me?"

Ana said, "No, come on. Everyone already knows how humiliated I am, anyway, so the more the merrier."

And half the school probably heard me say Blaine's name, too! Tears stung in Ana's eyes. *Now everyone really will think I'm chasing him!*

"What do you mean?" Barbie asked. "Is someone being mean to you?" She opened her purse, took out a pack of tissues, and handed one to Ana. Pink, of course, Ana noticed. Even in the middle of this total disaster, that was pretty funny. *Where does she get pink tissues?*

Nichelle sat down next to Ana and threw an arm over her shoulder. "Is it Blaine? 'Cause if it is, I'll knock his block off."

"Me, too!" said Barbie.

"You guys are the greatest. But I can handle it." Ana squeezed Nichelle's hand. "He's just nothing, compared to the track meet, anyway. It's the last big meet before the triathlon, and I swear I am going to win something."

"And I'll be there filming every minute!" Barbie said enthusiastically. Barbie had started joining Nichelle and Ana at the pool every morning, too. Swimming was a good way to keep from stressing about her acting auditions.

"Yeah, and I'll be there, too," Nichelle said.

Ana wiped her eyes with the tissue. "Thanks, you two."

The hallway had pretty much emptied out by now. Nobody wanted to hang around school after hours on a beautiful day like today. Lara shouted at them from the other end of the hall in her cute French accent. "*Allo! Allo!* Let's go get some french fries! Even if they are not French!" Being from Paris, Lara thought it was hysterical that they were called "french" fries.

"Okay, guys, Lara's right, let's move this thing along. Even I can't be serious forever," Ana said. "I want a cheeseburger, and nothing's going to stand in my way. I'll race you to Eatz!"

The four girls took off at full speed, running down the street, dodging businessmen and bike messengers. Ana pulled into the lead, hurdling up and over a bucket of roses the florist had set on the sidewalk.

"No fair!" Nichelle shouted. "You're a trained athlete!"

Barbie panted, "I'm going to start jogging again. Every day, I swear." In a sudden burst of energy, she swung herself forward into the lead as Ana slowed down to dodge a taxi.

Suddenly there was the sound of in-line skates coming up from behind. Tori blazed past all four runners, circling them several times. "Meet you at Eatz!" she shouted to them as she bladed on down the street.

They all met at the doorway to Eatz, laughing hysterically and gasping for breath.

"I don't think they'll even let us in," Nichelle said, surveying the group critically. "We are a sweaty, disgusting mess."

"Speak for yourself!" Ana and Barbie spoke together. Lara stuck out her tongue.

"Okay," Nichelle shrieked. "I am an utterly gorgeous, drop-dead vision of perfection! And you guys . . . are a sweaty, disgusting mess!" Then Nichelle ran through the door at Eatz, trying to stay ahead of Ana, Lara, and Barbie as they charged at her.

Tori was already standing at the counter, inside, balancing on her in-line skates. *She makes it look so easy*, Ana thought. Skating her way through the crowd, Tori balanced a giant plate of french fries in one hand and a Coke in the other. She pointed with her nose over to an empty booth.

Even I can't be a health nut all the time, Ana thought. *And those fries smell great!*

Ana forgot all her worries about Clarisse and Blaine, and spent the rest of the afternoon laughing with her friends. She even ordered a second basket of french fries.

* * * * * *

The next morning was Saturday, and Ana was at the track bright and early. She made sure she wore her lucky T-shirt over her I. H. top. Four other teams from all over the city were there for the meet. Thank goodness the I. H. team was running on its home track. Some of those teams looked fast!

She touched her lucky blue T-shirt as she always did. Her brother Juan had already left for Hawaii. But as long as she had the shirt, he was with her. Stretching in her usual routine, Ana felt terrific. *I really could win today! Look out, Clarisse, here I come.*

Ana felt bad for a second. She should just want to beat her own best time. But if she could beat Clarisse, too, well, that would just make her day complete. And then she could forget this whole Blaine thing for good.

She could see Barbie up on the bleachers, changing the battery on her video camera. Barbie looked casual today, wearing jeans and a baby blue sweater, with pink high-top sneakers. You have to move fast to film the action, Barbie always said. She filmed all of Ana's races. Ana would watch all the tapes later, trying to improve her running style. Barbie was great at finding the perfect camera angle.

And Nichelle sat next to Barbie, all bundled up in her favorite purple blazer. Nichelle always looked perfectly dressed, no matter where she was. *No wonder she's rising in the modeling world*, Ana thought. *Even sitting in the bleachers, she looks ready for a photo shoot.*

Ana laughed as Barbie poked Nichelle in the ribs with a cup of hot chocolate from a Thermos, and Nichelle made a face. Ana waved at them, and they waved back. She had such great friends. They were so sweet to blow a whole Saturday morning just to come to Ana's track meet.

Coach Arlen shouted for the team to gather around. Clarisse strolled lazily over from the locker room, tying her long red hair up in a dark green headband. Ana reminded herself that Clarisse wasn't as lazy as she looked. As a runner, she was hard to beat.

"Nice outfit, Ana," Clarisse said sneeringly, staring at Ana's lucky T-shirt. Clarisse's friend Tiffany giggled behind her hand.

Ana burned with annoyance. *Now I'm really going to beat you into the ground, Clarisse!*

"I run faster with this on," Ana said flatly. "I beat you in it before."

Clarisse's face reddened. "We'll see," she said.

Tiffany looked nervously at the two girls.

"Our opponents are the other teams, right?" Tiffany asked. "Right?"

Neither Ana nor Clarisse answered her. Just then, Clarisse's dad, dressed in an expensive cashmere coat, called to Clarisse from the sideline. Ana was jealous for a brief second. Her Papa's construction business kept him so busy that he didn't make it to her track meets very often. But her jealousy died quickly when she overheard what Clarisse's dad was saying.

"Clarisse, you'd better get serious this time," he said sternly. "Please don't let me down again."

Clarisse's ordinarily confident voice took on a defensive tone. "I got second place overall in the last meet, Daddy."

Ana remembered this all too well. Clarisse had run a phenomenal meet and had barely missed out on first place. Ana had placed third — and her parents had been thrilled!

"Second place is for losers," Clarisse's father said. "Nobody remembers the world's greatest second-place finishers," he went on mockingly. "I didn't make my fortune by coming in second to anyone, did I?"

"No, Daddy." Clarisse sounded miserable.

"So no more excuses. Just get in there and win! That's my girl!" He slapped Clarisse on the back once, and went back to the stands.

No wonder she's kind of mean, Ana thought shaking her head. Ana lined up at the blocks. As she began to focus, all her annoyances seemed to fade away. This was what it was all about. The race. All the training and practice finally narrowing down to a few seconds of pure, thrilling athletic joy.

Two lanes away, Ana could hear Clarisse muttering under her breath, "Excuses are for losers, excuses are for losers," over and over again. But Ana blocked it out. At least for this instant, Clarisse wasn't important at all.

Then the starting gun went off, and she was running. She could feel her legs pumping, and the track blurred by on each side. She heard footsteps behind her, and poured it on as hard as she could.

Ana crossed the line with a surge of surprise. It had seemed so quick. Coach Arlen was screaming and pounding her on the back.

"Ana, you won! You won a sprint!"

Ana's mouth hung open with disbelief. She knew she'd been getting better in her sprints, but she didn't think she'd win this event. Clarisse was a better sprinter! But Clarisse hadn't been training the way Ana had. She walked it out, breath coming heavy in her lungs. But she couldn't get the smile off her face. Barbie and Nichelle were both cheering in the stands.

Clarisse had come in second. The cloud on her face made it obvious, even if she hadn't heard the results. Clarisse's time had been good, too — the same time she had been beating Ana with in practice. It wasn't that she had gotten worse. It was that Ana had gotten better!

Ana saw Clarisse start to walk toward her father in the stands. But he turned his back as she approached, pointing back to the track. Ana was amazed to find herself actually feeling sorry for Clarisse, if only for a moment.

Back in the stands, Barbie and Nichelle were both still applauding as Blaine approached them. He was wearing an old striped rugby shirt and jeans with a tear in the knee. Blaine cleared his throat. Barbie stopped the camera abruptly.

"Hello, Blaine," Nichelle said coldly. "Are you here to watch Clarisse?"

"No, I'm here to find out what gives." Blaine's words spilled out quickly and nervously. "Ana and I were getting along great, I thought! And all of a sudden, she's giving me the evil eye. And you guys barely speak to me anymore.

"I really like Ana," he went on, "and I don't know what I did wrong to mess it up! I figured that since you guys are her best friends, you'd know what it was."

Nichelle and Barbie eyed each other. Finally Barbie spoke, "We don't know what happened. I figured you guys had a fight or something."

Nichelle agreed. "Ana won't explain it. And I shouldn't say this, but she really liked you, too. Then, all of a sudden — poof! — she isn't talking to you. So we aren't either."

"Is she like that usually?"

"Absolutely not!" Barbie answered. "So if you didn't have a fight, then something else happened. Ana doesn't do stuff without a reason."

"Are you totally and completely sure you weren't being a jerk?" Nichelle asked.

Blaine looked offended. "Not unless I have amnesia, and nobody told me! Would I be here this early on a Saturday if I was a jerk?"

Nichelle raised her hands in surrender, "Okay,

don't get your pants in a bunch. I had to ask. So what could it be?"

"When did she change?" Barbie asked.

Blaine thought back. "That day after history class. We had a great time in class, and then she went off to track practice. When I ran into her the next day, she walked by me like I didn't exist. Like she couldn't stand the sight of me!"

"So it was something at practice, because Ana goes straight home afterward. Do you have any old girlfriends on the track team? Maybe one of them said something," Barbie asked.

"No, I don't have any old girlfriends on the team." Blaine pushed his hair back awkwardly out of his face.

"Clarisse!" Nichelle exclaimed, sitting bolt upright. "It has to be her! You know she's jealous of Ana. And she's on the track team, too, so she had the motive and the opportunity."

"But Ana knows that, so why would she listen to anything Clarisse said about Blaine?" asked Barbie.

"Yes, and why would Clarisse say anything bad

about me?" Blaine asked. "She and I both went to the same school before we came to International High."

"Ha! So she was your girlfriend!" Nichelle said, like a TV attorney.

"No! I swear she wasn't," Blaine said, laughing. "The whole truth and nothing but the truth! I went to the movies with her a couple of times last year, and then it was over, but she still seems to think she owns me or something."

"Ah-HA!" said Barbie. "So she doesn't like it at all that you're interested in Ana."

"So, what if she dropped a little hint to Ana?" said Nichelle. "Like, 'Oh, Blaine doesn't really like you, he likes *me!*' There are lots of ways Clarisse could mess with Ana's mind."

"So all I have to do is convince Ana that whatever this bad thing Clarisse said is, it's totally bogus?"

"Right!" said Barbie.

"But she won't talk to me, so how can I do that?" Blaine beat on his leg with his fist in frustration. "Signal flags?"

"We'll help you," Barbie promised.

"Starting right now," Nichelle said. "Maybe she won't talk to you, but she can't stop hearing you if you cheer for her! The next race she runs, you shout her name!"

"She won't hear it during the race," Barbie said. "Let's start yelling now!"

Down on the track, Ana wasn't thinking about Blaine or Clarisse at all. She was sipping sports juice, watching another race and thinking about the triathlon coming up next month. It was going to be awesome, running with all those grown-up athletes in Central Park.

Suddenly she heard a shout from the stands. "Go, Ana," a boy's voice yelled. She turned around and looked. Blaine? What was Blaine doing here? Cheering for her, Ana realized!

Standing next to Blaine, Barbie and Nichelle were waving. Nichelle flashed her a huge smile and a thumbs-up sign. Blaine held his arms overhead in the championship salute. Without even thinking about it, Ana waved back at all of them. Maybe she'd been wrong about Blaine. And nobody could say she was chasing him — she hadn't even invited him to the meet, but he'd come anyway to root for her! One more win, and this day would be perfect.

Ana wasn't the only one who'd heard Blaine's yelling. Clarisse had heard it, too, and her face looked like a thundercloud. She threw her water bottle with an angry thud into the ice, and stamped past her friend Tiffany on the way to the starting blocks for the hurdles. Her father stood in silence on the sideline, waiting for her to win. "I'll show them," Clarisse muttered. "I'll show them all."

The girls lined up again at the starting blocks. Clarisse was right next to Ana this time, just one lane over to the right, and Tiffany was in the lane to her left. Ana turned to wish them both "good luck" automatically.

Tiffany answered back, "Good luck, you guys." Clarisse said nothing, in a serious eyes-front sulk. Tiffany was kind of nice, Ana thought. Even if she was Clarisse's best friend.

Blaine yelled again from the stands, "Go, Ana! Go for the gold!"

Tiffany said to Ana, "Nice-looking fan club you got there."

Pushing the Limits

Clarisse said rudely, "Just shut up and run, Tiffany." Tiffany looked hurt. Ana wondered what Clarisse's problem was. Usually she could at least manage being nice to Tiffany.

The girls braced themselves for the start, and then they were off! Ana felt that rush again. Today was her day, and she felt like she just couldn't lose. Ana knew that Barbie was filming her from the sideline, but she put it out of her mind. The race was all that mattered.

She approached the first hurdle and cleared it with a perfect running leap, landing without breaking stride, and pounded down the track. *I'm going to win again!* The hurdles flashed by underneath, and Ana was in the home stretch. Clarisse was right on her heels, Ana could hear her familiar footsteps. *Don't blow it now!*

Clarisse was catching up! Ana could hear the footsteps getting closer and closer. Then Clarisse was even with her! She was pulling ahead of Ana, one inch at a time. Clarisse was going to win.

Ana refused to give up, remembering what Clarisse had said in the locker room about her and Blaine. *I bet she knew I was there all along!* A burst of energy welled up inside her. Ana ran harder than she ever had in her life. She pulled even with Clarisse, and they ran side by side for an instant. Then Ana was the one pulling ahead, leaning forward to run even faster.

I've got it! This race is mine! She heard Blaine and Nichelle cheering, "Ana, Ana!"

Suddenly Ana felt herself falling! She stumbled, desperately trying to maintain her footing, but she couldn't. The hard ground of the track knocked the wind out of her as she collapsed. And she had been so close! Bitter disappointment filled her. *Those were the best hurdles I've ever run! Well, they would have been, if I'd just gotten across the finish line.*

Ana could feel her knee bleeding where she'd scraped it. What a great thing for Barbie to catch on film! A movie called, *Ana falls flat on her face!*

Well, no point in sitting here in the dirt all day. Ana brushed herself off and stood up. Or tried to stand up! Her ankle screamed with pain when she put her weight on it.

"Oh, no!" Ana whispered. "Not with the triathlon coming in three weeks. I've been training for over a year!" But it was true. Her ankle was already swelling. She'd blown her chance for the triathlon.

Nichelle and Blaine were climbing down from the bleachers toward Ana. But Barbie, who'd been filming from the finish line, got there first.

"Ana, that was a terrible fall! Are you all right?" Barbie slung her backpack over her shoulder to give Ana an arm to lean on.

"I've hurt my ankle," Ana said, swallowing the lump in her throat. *I will not cry! I will not. Not even in front of Barbie.*

"Oh, no." Barbie stared at Ana in dismay. She knew how important this was.

Nichelle and Blaine ran up, next to the coach.

Coach Arlen spoke first. "Ana, are you okay? Do you want to have the doctor look at it?"

"That was some spill you took, Ana," Nichelle said. "What happened?"

"I don't know. I just don't know."

Nichelle and Barbie helped Ana over to the bench. Blaine ran to get an ice pack.

Her ankle was throbbing now, hurting worse

than ever. Blaine held the ice pack on it gently. Coach Arlen examined it, shaking her head grimly.

"It may just be a sprain, Ana. But it could be broken." She flexed the hurt ankle.

Ana wailed in protest, more from the bad news than from the pain. "It can't be broken!"

"The doctor will let you know for sure."

The crowd clapped as Ana was helped off the field.

"So who won the race?" Ana asked Barbie.

"Clarisse," Barbie answered. "But you'd have won if you hadn't fallen."

"Burn this tape, will you, Barbie? This is one race I would love to forget!"

Chapter 6

Barbie's Instant Replay

On the sideline, Barbie, Nichelle, and Blaine watched the rest of the meet while the team doctor was taping up Ana's ankle. Clarisse tore up the track, winning event after event. Barbie was happy for the I. H. team but, just the same, she couldn't help feeling a bit depressed. She felt that Ana should be out there sharing in the glory. What bad luck!

"You know, for someone who's winning everything, Clarisse doesn't look happy," Barbie observed.

"Oh, who knows what that girl's problem is?"

Nichelle said. "Ask me if I care, after the way she's treated Ana."

Barbie sighed. Why was high school so difficult sometimes? She looked down at her video camera. It was a good thing it had an instant playback function. At least she could use it to look at Ana's races. She knew Ana wanted her to erase it, but Tori would kill her if she didn't at least look for a couple of good pictures for the web page.

Barbie rewound the cassette and started looking at the images in the tiny playback window. She replayed the first race, and there was a perfect picture of Ana's smiling face as she crossed the finish line. That would look great on the web page! The shot of Clarisse finishing second looked good, too. Action shots were the best!

As the tape rolled on, Barbie watched in the viewfinder as Ana readied herself for the second race. Barbie hated watching, knowing how it would end. As the key part of the race came up, just before Ana fell, Barbie studied the tape closely. First, Ana was ahead. Then Clarisse came up even with Ana, and the two of them were running so close together that they were practically touching each other. Ana pulled ahead by one step. Clarisse fought to keep up. On the audio, Barbie could hear Nichelle and Blaine cheering, screaming Ana's name.

Then — bang! Ana was lying on the track again, in obvious pain. It all happened so fast that Barbie could only see a tangle of arms and legs.

Barbie rewound the tape again.

"What are you doing?" Nichelle asked. "Isn't it bad enough watching Ana fall twice? Do you have to see it again?"

"I'm trying to figure out why she fell," Barbie said. She wrinkled her forehead and stared into the tiny playback window. This time she ran the tape frame by frame, paying close attention to Ana's feet. Suddenly an unexpected movement caught her eye on the tape. It wasn't Ana's feet. It was Clarisse's left arm. It was swinging up and over into Ana's lane, hitting Ana's elbow and pitching her forward. Then Ana stumbled and went down.

Barbie felt sick. It must have been an accident.

It had to have been. She watched the tape two more times, trying to prove it was just a mistake. But the videotape didn't lie. Clarisse had reached out and shoved Ana! There was no way it was an accident.

"Hello, Earth to Barbie!" Nichelle had been trying to get Barbie's attention for a while. "What's so fascinating in there?"

Barbie almost wished she hadn't seen the tape, that she had erased it like Ana had asked her to. But she couldn't do that now. Clarisse had cheated to win the race. And Ana was wiped out of the triathlon because of it. What was she supposed to do now?

Both Blaine and Nichelle were staring at Barbie now. "What's up, chick?" Nichelle said.

Barbie pointed at the tiny playback screen, frozen on the end of the race. She handed Nichelle the video camera. "Watch Clarisse's arms right before Ana falls," Barbie said, "and please, please tell me I'm just seeing things."

Nichelle watched in silence. Then she whistled softly. She handed the video camera to Blaine, and he watched it, too.

"Tell me I'm wrong," Barbie pleaded with both of them. "Tell me it isn't what it looks like."

"Clarisse shoved her on purpose." Nichelle was outraged. "That no-good, worthless, rotten little . . . I can't even think of a low enough word for her!"

Down on the track, the last race of the day was just beginning. Coach Arlen was helping Ana, her ankle now heavily bandaged, walk across the field on crutches toward her friends in the bleachers.

"What are we going to do?" Barbie said.

Nichelle spotted Ana limping up the steps and got even madder. "I'll go right to Principal Simmons. I'll go to Coach Arlen. I'll get her butt bounced right out of International High!"

"Nichelle, we have to tell Ana." Barbie spoke firmly. "She's the one who got hurt. She should decide what to do."

Blaine agreed. "We have to, Nichelle. I can't believe Clarisse was such a total rat!"

Nichelle said in an awed tone of voice, "Wow, and you think I'm mad! Ana's been training for the Central Park Triathlon for almost a year.

And Clarisse pulls this garbage! Ana's going to kill her."

All three of them sat in silence as Ana limped her way over to them.

"Man, what rotten luck!" Ana said, slumping down on a bleacher seat. Nichelle and Blaine moved over to make room for her. "The doctor says I've got a really bad sprain. Of all the lousy times to fall down." She was trying to sound tough, but her voice was quavery with tears. "With the triathlon only three weeks away."

Barbie said, "Ana . . . I . . . ," and then broke off in confusion. Nichelle put an arm around Ana and hugged her.

Finally it was Blaine who handed Ana the video camera. "It wasn't bad luck. Look at this!"

Ana watched the tape play. She braced herself, waiting to see herself fall. But what she saw instead was even worse.

Ana exploded, "She pushed me! She pushed me on purpose so she would win!"

"We're going to take this right to Coach Arlen," Nichelle said. "She'll be off the team so fast, her head will spin."

"And to Principal Simmons, too," Blaine added.

Ana handed the video camera back to Barbie. "Great. Let's do it right now. Embarrass her in front of everyone!" She'd never been angrier than she was right this second. She'd been training for a year, and Clarisse had wrecked it in ten seconds! Her ankle was twice its normal size and throbbed with pain. "She deserves what's coming to her!"

But as Ana began to work her way down the steps, she bumped into Clarisse's dad. He was intently watching the last race on the field and didn't realize he was blocking the way. *Clarisse is winning another one*, Ana thought sourly. *It helps when you remove the competition.*

"Oh, excuse me," he said absently, never taking his eyes off his daughter down on the track. Then he focused on Ana. "You're the young lady who was hurt! You're quite a runner!" His eyes returned to Clarisse on the track. "That's my little girl down there," he said, pointing her out. "Isn't she amazing? I knew she had it in her to win, with the proper motivation."

Oh, yeah, you gave her the proper motivation! If you'd motivated her any more, she'd have broken my leg to win the race.

A well-dressed woman in her forties was coming up the stairs toward them. "Oh, honey," Clarisse's dad said, "this is one of Clarisse's teammates."

The woman — Clarisse's mom — ignored Ana totally. "Did she win?"

He smiled proudly. "She won! She's going to be first overall!"

"That's my baby!" Now that the race was over, the runners were heading for their friends and families in the stands.

Nichelle poked Ana in the back, indicating Clarisse, who was walking with Coach Arlen toward them. Ana opened her mouth to say something. She could point Clarisse out as a cheater right now and end this. She took a deep breath to do it.

As she did, Clarisse's father opened his arms to Clarisse. "Our little winner deserves a giant hug!" He enfolded Clarisse in his arms, and her mother did, too. "Are we proud, or are we proud?"

Clarisse's face lit up with the biggest smile Ana had ever seen on her.

Ana closed her mouth with a snap. Blaine looked at her inquiringly. She shook her head. Not in front of her parents. Clarisse deserved it, for sure, but Ana just couldn't do it.

But, oh, it hurt to see Coach Arlen congratulate Clarisse on her performance, with Ana sitting on the sideline. Maybe she could just tell the coach. But what if she did? She'd boot Clarisse off the team in a heartbeat. And with Ana out with a bad ankle and Clarisse kicked off, the team would be right out of the finals. Ana ground her teeth. It wasn't fair!

"Tell her," Nichelle urged in a harsh whisper. "Tell the coach! She doesn't deserve to be standing up there getting a stinking trophy!"

Ana shook her head stubbornly. "It'll mess up the team if I do. I'll settle Clarisse my own way."

"How?" Barbie said.

"I don't know yet," Ana said. "But I'll think of something. Hang on to that tape, will you?"

"I will," Barbie promised. "It'll be ready when you need it."

Chapter 7

Adding Insult to Injury

Ana let herself sink into the pool. Ahhh! It was such a relief to take the weight off her ankle. But she couldn't swim worth anything with the ankle brace on. So she just used her arms, dragging herself through the water. It was better than nothing.

Well, at least she'd have more time for all her friends since she was off the track team for a month. The swimming would help her keep in shape for the swim team in the spring. And she should probably be studying more, too, particularly for Mr. Budge's exam. Why did she have to end up with the toughest teacher in the whole school? At least it was just American history, so there was only about two hundred years of it. Ana crossed her eyes and made a face thinking about it. Memorizing dates and battles, ick!

"Hey, Blaine!" Ana yelled over the concrete edge of the pool. "Have you started studying for history yet?"

Blaine was sitting with his textbook open, but his eyes were closed and he was faking a snore.

"Verrrry funny, Blaine." Ana laughed despite herself. "Have you ever thought about stand-up comedy?"

Blaine opened his eyes and said, "Oh, sure. Right. Particularly when my parents laugh at my report card. My dad will not be amused if I blow history."

Ana smiled. Blaine cracked her up. And the fact that he was way cute didn't hurt, either. "Do you want to study together?" she asked.

Blaine faked a sword stab through the heart. "I would die for the chance!"

"You'll probably wish you were dead when you see my notes. I haven't been paying attention at all for weeks!"

Ana had been trying to stay cheerful and up-beat, but it was awfully hard sometimes. Later that day, she sat by herself in Mr. Toussaint's empty classroom. Her crutches were propped awkwardly against the next desk. Her ankle was wrapped in a giant stiff brace, and it ached when she walked. Usually, she'd have been at practice right now, lacing up her sneakers and stretching. Or biking around the bike track, trying to speed up her time. But that was through for her. Done, finished, gone!

And what's worse, she hadn't thought of a way to get Clarisse back that wouldn't mess up things for the team. Not like Clarisse had been getting in Ana's face the way she had before. If anything, it seemed like she had been trying to avoid Ana. But that didn't make it right!

Ana swallowed around a lump in her throat. *I will not feel sorry for myself. I will not! Lots of people have bigger problems than this.* But the tears welled up in her eyes, anyway, as she looked down for the tenth time at the announcement she'd gotten in the mail that morning, confirming her registration in the Central Park Triathlon. *It's too late now*, Ana thought. And she couldn't even get the entry fee back, either! Her parents had been so disappointed, too. Ana had wanted to tell them the whole story. But she knew if she did, her father would come down to the school in a rage and insist that the school kick Clarisse off the team.

Blaine pushed the classroom door open and stuck his head in. "Can I come in?"

"Sure, Blaine." That was the only good thing to come out of this whole nightmare. She knew Blaine really did like her. If he was willing to put up with her on crutches, losing her temper every five seconds at every little thing, he must like her a lot!

"You're writing for *Generation Beat*, aren't you?" Blaine asked.

"Well, I was going to write an article about the triathlon. But that's kind of pointless now." Ana swung herself up on her crutches. Blaine shouldered her backpack for her. "Thanks for all your help," she said. "But I'm heading out to the track."

"Seriously? But I thought there was . . . ," he broke off awkwardly.

"No hope of the triathlon?"

Blaine's face fell.

Ana reassured him, "It's okay, I don't mind talking about it. The doctor says I have about a five percent chance of being able to do it."

"Ana, that's awesome!"

"No, that's a ninety-five percent chance that it won't happen. But I've got three weeks for my ankle to get better. If all I can do is swim with a brace on, then that's what I'll do. But Coach Arlen has some rehab ideas she wants to try out on me. So I'm going to try it."

Ana walked, or rather limped, out across the track toward Coach Arlen. Suddenly she paused. Clarisse was standing out there next to her!

Clarisse turned around as Ana approached, her face flushed and angry. Or was she upset? Had Coach Arlen somehow found out what Clarisse had done? Had Clarisse confessed? Maybe Ana wouldn't have to do anything at all.

And if Clarisse got kicked off the team, it wouldn't be Ana's fault.

But as soon as Coach Arlen spoke, Ana knew she'd been wrong. Clarisse was upset, but the coach wasn't.

"Ana, I've had a wonderful idea," the coach began. "I've got a whole schedule of rehab exercises for you to do, and I think they'll really help. But since I'm going to be gone for ten days at the coaches' conference, Clarisse has volunteered to help you train. Isn't that great?"

Ana wanted to scream. Coach Arlen was a great coach, but there were times she could be so utterly clueless. And, looking at Clarisse's face, it was clear that she hadn't "volunteered" to do anything.

It was almost funny, in a sick and twisted way. Clarisse looked so uncomfortable. *"Guilty conscience bothering you, Clarisse?"* Ana wanted to say. And Clarisse probably had no idea that Ana knew what she had done! Well, let her suffer. Ana would kill her with kindness . . . at least until she could think of something better!

"That is so sweet of you, Clarisse," Ana said in

the nicest voice she could manage under the circumstances. "I couldn't think of anyone I'd rather have help me recover!"

"Clarisse will work with you every day until I get back," Coach Arlen said brightly. "Won't you, Clarisse?"

Clarisse looked like she was about to throw up. "Absolutely, Coach. Happy to help a teammate."

Ana, remembering that Clarisse hated early morning track meets, made a suggestion. "I train every morning, starting at six A.M. Is that good for you, Clarisse?"

"Oh sure," Clarisse said glumly. "That'll be just fine."

"That's my girls!" Coach Arlen said. "Now I can leave for the conference knowing everything's in good hands."

✳ ✳ ✳ ✳ ✳ ✳

At Eatz, later that day, Ana sprang the news.

Nichelle nearly choked on a french fry. "Get out — she's your coach?"

"Sure, Ana." Clarisse got out of the pool, shivered, and went to get Ana's bag.

Ana felt almost mean when she saw how quickly Clarisse did everything she said. It wasn't as much fun as she'd thought. And Clarisse turned out to be a really good coach, which made it worse. But she wasn't letting her off the hook, either. "We're meeting again for more training right after school, right?"

"Is that what you do?" Clarisse asked.

"Every day."

Clarisse sighed. "Then that's what we'll do. I guess."

Ana was sure Clarisse would slack off after a couple of days. But to Ana's amazement, she didn't. She was there every morning. And she really was a ton of help, even though Ana treated her like a total servant. Clarisse knew tricks to help Ana keep weight off her bad ankle so she wasn't reinjuring it by walking around. Whatever else she might have done, Ana realized, Clarisse was a terrific athlete.

By the fifth day, Ana had almost forgotten that she was just doing this to torment Clarisse. The exercises seemed to be working. And her ankle was getting a little bit better.

Clarisse was starting to take the coaching bit seriously. She was showing up ready to train, instead of half asleep and resentful. And whenever Ana slacked off, Clarisse got right in her face about it. *She's starting to sound like Coach Arlen*, Ana realized.

"Planning on sleeping through the triathlon, are we?" Clarisse would say, handing Ana some water. And Ana would get up and keep going, if only to prove Clarisse wrong. Ana was swimming more laps than she ever had before, and walking in the pool to strengthen her ankle. After a week, Ana started biking again. Her ankle was sore and stiff, but she could do it.

It was the running that scared Ana the most. Clarisse had her walking around the track so slowly! She would never be ready to run the triathlon in time. Finally, on the last day before Coach Arlen was due back, Ana finally blew up.

"I just can't do it, Clarisse." Ana was almost yelling as she trudged around the track. "I'm tired, and I'm sick of this! I don't get enough sleep, all I do is train, and it's all for nothing. Nothing! My ankle is not going to make it, and neither am I!"

Clarisse stopped running backward in front of Ana. "I don't get enough sleep, either," she yelled back. "I've been getting up at five A.M. for you, and you are going to make it if it kills both of us!"

"There's only one week left! One week, and I haven't even been able to run yet."

"Then today's the day," Clarisse said. "Look down at the other end of the track."

Ana did. "There's nothing there!"

"Yes there is. There's the big ice-cream sundae I'm going to buy you at Eatz when you run a lap around this track."

"Clarisse, that is the stupidest thing I've ever heard."

"So do you want the sundae or not?" Clarisse said mockingly, and started jogging slowly forward. "Run one lap, and then I couldn't care less. Be a couch potato if you want. Go watch *Melrose Place* if you want to be a lazy quitter!"

How dare she call me a lazy quitter? After what she did to me! She would have said it, but Clarisse was already running down the track.

Ana started to run then. Not very fast, but definitely running. Her ankle ached, and her whole body felt creaky. But she was running! *I'll show her a lazy quitter!*

Clarisse slowed down to let Ana catch up as they crossed the finish line.

"See, I knew you could run," Clarisse said smugly. "You should thank me."

Ana was beyond outrage. "Oh, yeah, thank you for calling me a lazy quitter! After what you did?"

"What?" Clarisse said.

"You heard me!" Ana grabbed her backpack up from the bench. "I've got something to show you, Clarisse."

"I don't know what you mean."

"Let me give you a little clue. Barbie films all of my races."

Ana walked into the gym and popped the tape into the VCR the football coach used to replay the games. The audio was broken, but they didn't need it. The tape played in total silence.

"Well?"

Clarisse said nothing. She stared numbly at the screen.

Ana had thought she would feel excited about this. Making Clarisse admit what she'd done. But it wasn't as much fun as she'd thought.

Clarisse had been a good coach, too. And remembering how Clarisse's father had spoken, Ana wondered if maybe Clarisse actually thought calling Ana a "lazy quitter" was a good way to motivate her.

Clarisse's face was white. "I never meant for you to get hurt, Ana, I swear. I know you don't believe that, but it's true. I just wanted to win so much." She went on, almost crying. "I heard Blaine yell your name, and I was so jealous. I thought if I won, he'd notice me instead of you. And my dad thinking I was such a loser if I didn't come in first. You don't know what he's like when I lose a race."

"So you knocked me down on purpose!"

"The second after I did it, I knew I shouldn't have. But I just kept running, and then Coach Arlen was slapping me on the back. I wanted to tell her, but I just couldn't. And then Mom and Dad were clapping when I got the trophy, and I wanted to tell them to stop, but I couldn't get the words out. Dad said he was proud of me." Clarisse's voice broke a little. "He never says that."

Clarisse went on, "And then, when Coach Arlen said I had to help you train, it was even worse. I just felt so sick every time I saw you on crutches. When did you find out?"

"Right after the race, when Barbie played back the tape." Ana had been so angry then, ready to get Clarisse kicked off the team. Even kicked out of school. But now she was almost starting to feel sorry for her.

"You knew right then? Even when my parents were there ? . . . and you didn't say anything?"

"It didn't seem like a good time."

"I didn't deserve the trophy. I wanted to throw it out, but Dad took it to his office. Look, Ana, I know you hate me. I'll resign from the team."

"No, Clarisse. The team needs you. You're the best runner we've got. And" — Ana cleared her throat — "I need you, too."

"What?" Clarisse asked.

"You're the best coach I've ever had. Coach Arlen is going to be too busy to work with me every day. And it was only because you made me so mad just now that I was able to run."

Clarisse stared at Ana. "So you still want me as your coach?"

Ana thought about it. "Yeah, believe it or not, I do. Will you do it?"

"Yeah. And, Ana?"

"What?"

"I know you're not a lazy quitter."

Both girls laughed. "Thanks for nothing, Clarisse."

"You're welcome for nothing!" Clarisse said. "Tell me something, did you work out at six every day before this, or was that just to make me suffer?"

Ana laughed. "Not until seven. And I've been suffering along with you." Ana had been punishing herself, too, when she thought about it. She'd been getting up everyday before the sun was even up just so Clarisse would have to get up, too.

"You're running extra laps for that! And can we please start at seven tomorrow?" Clarisse asked plaintively.

"You're on . . . Coach."

The two girls shook hands. If someone had told Ana two weeks ago that she and Clarisse could end up being friends, she wouldn't have believed it. Well, maybe she was going a little too far. At least, they weren't enemies.

Chapter 8

The Big Day

The morning of the triathlon, the sky looked like rain. Ana had been too nervous to sleep, but she wasn't tired. She'd gotten up early to meet Clarisse at the school track.

"Got everything?" Clarisse asked. Nichelle, Barbie, Tori, Lara, Chelsie, and Blaine were meeting them in Central Park in twenty minutes.

"Bathing suit, check. Bike, check. Cross-trainers and running shorts, check. Everything except my sanity!"

Ana couldn't believe today was the day. By dinnertime tonight, it would all be over.

"You'll be fine," Clarisse said. "Better than fine."

Ana turned to her. She didn't want to say it, but she felt obligated to. "Clarisse, I couldn't have done this without you."

"Listen, Ana . . . ," Clarisse began. "I know we've been working together and all, but you don't have to pretend to be nice. You can still hate me if you want. I'd have hated you if you had done it."

"So maybe I'm not you, okay? Forget about it — this time."

Clarisse shot Ana a look.

Ana met her eyes and went on, "I mean it, Clarisse. If you ever do something like that again, I'm going to knock your block off. But it's done. Forgotten."

Clarisse went on, as if Ana hadn't said anything. "You can trip me at the next track meet if you want. Seriously, I wish you would."

It was a stupid idea. But somehow Ana knew that Clarisse meant what she said.

"It's forgiven, Clarisse. Nobody gets tripped." It was one thing to say it. But could she really forgive her? Three weeks ago, Ana would have said, "Never." But now? Clarisse really had helped her more than anybody, even if it had only been because she felt guilty. Nobody else would have gotten up at 5:00 A.M. every day to swim with her. Or stayed late after school every day to run and bike. Or put up with Ana when she wanted to give up.

Ana looked at her watch. "Well, I guess we'd better get going, Coach."

Clarisse stuck out her hand, "I wouldn't miss it for the world. But you'd better do well."

"Excuse me?" Ana said.

"I said you'd better do well. I've got a reputation as a coach to uphold, you know."

Ana couldn't believe it! Clarisse actually had the nerve to speak to her like that. Then she realized Clarisse was hiding a grin.

"Just kidding, Ana," she said.

"I knew that," Ana said.

"Did not."

"Did too!"

The two girls left the I. H. track, heading for Central Park.

* * * * * *

At Central Park, Barbie, Nichelle, Chelsie, and Lara were already waiting for them in the tiny parking lot. A crowd had started to gather, even though the triathlon wouldn't start for more than an hour. The skies had cleared up, and it was a beautiful sunny day. Ana shivered with excitement.

Tori zoomed up on her in-line skates as Clarisse and Ana got off their bikes. She yelled in her unmistakable Australian accent, "Hey, there she is, the winner and new champion, Ana Suarez!" All around them, heads turned. Nobody could ever describe Tori as quiet!

Lara and Nichelle both laughed. "So are you ready to rock and roll?" Nichelle said.

"As ready as I'll ever be, Nichelle. Thanks to my coach here," Ana said, pointing to Clarisse.

From the way Nichelle was looking at Clarisse, Ana could tell that it was going to take Nichelle a

100

while to forgive her. Nichelle was a true-blue friend. Anybody who messed with a friend of Nichelle's did so at their peril.

"Quick, quick, everyone," Lara said, clapping her hands. "Let's pose for Barbie. Ana, put on your T-shirt!"

Ana was wearing her lucky T-shirt for the actual race, but she pulled on her official Central Park Triathlon T-shirt over it for the picture. All the girls posed for the digital camera. "Another one for the web page! Everybody smile!" said Barbie.

Everybody smiled. Blaine shouted to them from the parking lot, "Wait! Wait! There's someone else who wants to be in the picture."

It was Ana's mama! And her little sister, Rosa. And Papa! Ana couldn't believe it! Mama was so traditional, she didn't even approve of Ana doing school sports. But she had come all the way from Washington Heights to see Ana run the triathlon.

"Mama, you're really here!" Ana said in Spanish.

"And where else would I be? My daughter's crazy enough to do this stuff, then I'm crazy enough to come watch it!" She squeezed her daughter's arm and spoke into her ear. "I am so proud of you, my little Ana. I don't always say so, but I am."

Then she turned to her daughter's friends and spoke awkwardly in English. "It is very good to meet my daughter's friends."

"It's good to meet you, too, Mrs. Suarez," Barbie said, in Spanish. Ana stared at her friend. Barbie whispered to Ana, "Don't look so surprised, Goofy. I did grow up in California, you know."

Mrs. Suarez beamed as Barbie snapped a picture of Ana hugging Rosa, and then a group shot of everyone, with little Rosa sitting on Blaine's shoulders. The crowd around them had doubled already, with friends and families of all the competitors taking pictures and checking gear.

Then it was time to start. All her friends had to go stand over with the spectators. Clarisse said, "Good luck," and then she had to leave, too. *It's just me now!* thought Ana, as she started her stretches.

Barbie, Nichelle, Chelsie, Tori, and Lara were up in the stands, jumping up and down. Blaine was clearing off the front-row seats he'd saved for

Mama, Papa, and Rosa. Swimming was first, and they knew Ana was a great swimmer.

Ana threw herself into the water with a sense of relief. Maybe her jitters would go away once she started moving. And it was only a 1.5-kilometer swim, which was not so bad. She wished there was more swimming and less running. She shivered a little, less from the cold water than from the thought of the tough course ahead when the swimming was over.

But before she had time to worry any more, the whistle blew. The swimmers were off, splashing through the icy water. And it went like a dream. All those weeks of swimming with just her arms had made her stronger. She felt like a seal, cutting through the water. Her time was outstanding. She pulled herself out of the water and waved to her little sister. *I'm doing it, I'm doing the triathlon!* She dried off and threw on her bike shorts. *Keep moving!*

Ana got on her bike. Her legs shook from nervousness. It was weird: She rode all the time, even if it wasn't her strongest sport, but it was different being up here with all these serious-looking grown-up athletes. And it was a long, forty-kilo-meter bike ride, too. Almost twenty-five miles!

Ana pinned her number — 45 — on the back of her shirt. Her ankle was strapped up tight with tape, which was the best she could do. She was ready.

Ana stopped feeling nervous the moment the start gun went off. Nothing to do but ride! The breeze was in her face, and the spectators cheering along the route were just a blur of noise and color. Cycling wasn't Ana's strongest event, so she was glad it was in the middle, and not last. She settled into a nice, steady pace in the middle of the pack, loving the feel of the pedals moving smoothly under her feet. This event she couldn't win, not at this distance. The competition in her age group was pretty tough! But she could make up time swimming and running — if her ankle held up and she could run.

Ana knew she should spare her ankle as much as she could. But when a woman with a Columbia University sweatshirt and a red ponytail passed her going around a turn, cutting dangerously close to Ana's tires, she knew she was going to try to beat her! She pedaled furiously, burning up the track. But the woman just pedaled faster and faster, staying ahead of Ana. Ana focused on that ponytail ahead of her and pedaled harder than she ever had before. And then she was past her, racing down the home stretch and across the finish line. As she hopped off her bike, Blaine brought her a sports bottle full of water, and Ana drained it dry in two gulps.

"That was great!" Blaine said, smiling broadly. "Does your ankle hurt?"

"No," Ana lied. "It feels just fine." But it didn't. The extra effort Ana had put into beating Ms. Ponytail had made her ankle ache. But there wasn't any point in complaining.

Clarisse flashed the thumbs-up signal as she came back over from the officials. "Ana, you were awesome. They've got you tenth in your age group for the cycling event. That's way better than we'd thought you'd do with the cycling. Is the ankle okay?"

"Sure, Clarisse, it's fine." It throbbed with pain right as she said it.

But the last event was the run: Ten kilometers, or

six and two-tenths miles. Ordinarily, Ana could have run it without a problem. She even would have looked forward to it. But now? Her ankle was already swelling — she could feel it. If any of her friends saw it, they'd stop her from running.

But Ana wasn't going to quit now. Clarisse was screaming from the sideline, "Third! You're ranked third overall in your age group!" Wow! She really had done well in the swimming, if her overall ranking was that high.

No time to enjoy it, though. Ana was off on her run. She picked a slow, steady rhythm, trying to warm up. People were passing her on both sides. She sighed, hating the sight. But they would get tired eventually, and she'd get her shot; ten kilometers wasn't a sprint.

At kilometer four, Ana picked up her pace. Picked it up a lot! She could feel the energy change around her, feeling people become more focused. Ahead of her, she saw Ms. Ponytail again. *Time to make my move!* Suddenly, Ana realized why she wanted to beat the runner with the red ponytail so much. With her red hair and designer sneakers, she reminded her of Clarisse! She suppressed a grin.

Clarisse was motivating her even when she wasn't running against her. *Oh well, whatever works!*

Ana passed her, and was running faster and faster, when it happened. Suddenly her ankle popped under her, with a grinding sound. It hurt worse than anything Ana had ever felt. She gritted her teeth, holding back a cry of pain. But she didn't fall and she didn't stop running. Soon, Ms. Ponytail passed Ana and receded into the distance. Ana wanted to cry. She wanted to yell and scream. But she didn't. She just kept on running.

By kilometer eight, Ana felt like she was going to throw up every time her foot touched the ground. *Two more kilometers. I can take it for that long. Maybe.*

In the stands, Barbie worriedly studied Ana's face through binoculars. "She looks hurt."

"It's her ankle, it's got to be." Clarisse pounded her fist in her palm. "This is my fault."

"Maybe she should quit," Blaine said.

"Ana won't quit," Nichelle and Clarisse said in unison. Then they glared at each other.

"It's true," Tori agreed. "Ana will hop on one foot if she has to. But she'll finish that race."

Barbie said, "I've got an idea." She told it to everyone. "Are you with me?"

Down on the track, Ana came around the curve for the last time. She just didn't think she could make it. No one was going to be impressed if she crawled in on her hands and knees. *I shouldn't have tried. It was just too much for me.*

But as she ran by the stands, there was a giant shout. "You can do it, Ana!" It was Blaine and Nichelle, Barbie and Tori, Chelsie and Lara, Clarisse yelling her heart out, and her whole family screaming. Her mama's and papa's voices cut across the rest. "Run, Ana! Run!"

And Ana ran. Ran even though she didn't think she could. And all of a sudden, she knew she could do it. She could do anything! She crossed the finish line two steps ahead of the girl with the red ponytail, and shouted in triumph. Barbie was there with her video camera.

"So how was it?" Barbie asked in her best reporter style.

Ana looked down, and then over at the crowd of runners still crossing the finish line. She was sweaty and dirty. Her ankle was twice its normal size, and she was more tired than she'd ever been. She should be miserable. But she couldn't stop smiling!

"It was great! It was the greatest thing in my whole life!" And the strangest thing of all was that it was true. "Every minute of it!"

Then her friends surrounded her, laughing and cheering. Blaine poured water on her. Nichelle and Clarisse were giving her high fives. Mama, Papa, and Rosa were right there, her papa wiping tears from his eyes. "That's my daughter," he kept saying, introducing Ana to total strangers. "That's my little girl!"

"Papa, you're embarrassing me." Ana laughed. But she didn't mind. On a day like today, she didn't mind anything.

Clarisse came back from the officials. Everyone quieted down. Ana knew she had blown her ranking with the running. She had been so slow!

Clarisse cleared her throat in the sudden silence. "I'm pleased to inform you . . . ," she began, "that Ms. Ana Suarez is ranked . . . ," she paused for dramatic effect.

"Tell us already," Nichelle said.

"Is ranked . . ." She paused again.

"*Clarisse!*" Barbie said in frustration.

"Number nine in her age group!" Clarisse said triumphantly.

"Top ten!" Ana screamed. "I made top ten!" Even with her ankle, she had done it. "Next year, I'll be first for sure." She hugged Mama.

"Well, I don't know about that," Clarisse said. "Next year, I'm going to be doing the triathlon, too!" Everybody laughed.

"Well, at least I'll have someone to practice with," Ana said. She looked around at all her friends and felt tears well up in her eyes. Happy tears, this time.

"I'll never forget this year," Ana said. "Not as long as I live."

"Me neither," Blaine said. And suddenly, right there in front of everyone, Blaine leaned forward and kissed Ana! It was on the cheek, technically, but it was *really* close.

"Blaine Gordon!" Ana said, blushing. *My first kiss, and it was right in front of everyone!*

"Oooooh," Rosa sang out, "Blaine and Ana, sitting in a tree, K-I-S-S-I-N-G."

110

"Rosa, you shut up," Ana said. But Nichelle and Clarisse were both singing it now, and Tori, Barbie, Lara, and Chelsie all chimed in. Papa looked disapproving, and started to take a step forward, but Mama put a hand on his arm to stop him. She was laughing, Ana realized.

"Nice friends you have," Blaine said. He was blushing, too.

"The best friends in the whole world," Ana said. "Which is why I'm going to regret killing them if they don't quit singing this second!"

* * * * * *

Back at school on Monday, Ana was studying in the computer room with Blaine, Barbie, Nichelle, Lara, and Clarisse for Tuesday's history test. Nichelle and Clarisse were still not exactly buddies, but even Nichelle had to admit that Clarisse knew her history.

Tori burst in through the door at her customary breakneck speed, with her long blond hair flying behind her. "I've got ten minutes before biology," she said. "Just came to show you the triathlon pictures on the web page."

Tori brought up the web page on a computer, and there it was: Ana crossing the finish line of the Central Park Triathlon, her arms thrown in the air in triumph. "Some smile you got there, Ms. Suarez," Tori said. "And I like the article, too. Particularly the end."

As Blaine leaned in close to her, Ana read her own words on the screen:

"When I first started training for the triathlon, I thought it would be impossible. I pushed myself to my limits and beyond, before the triathlon even started. When I hurt my ankle, I wanted to quit. I didn't see how I could go on. But I did. When I wanted to give up, my friends, my family, and my track teammate and personal coach, Clarisse, were behind me, pushing me over that hill. It was a day I'll never forget as long as I live. It changed my life. So whatever you do, push yourself to the limit! You never know how far you'll go until you try."

Ana María Suarez

TURN THE PAGE TO CATCH
THE LATEST BUZZ FROM
THE *GENERATION BEAT* NEWSPAPER

I. H. STUDENT TRAINS FOR TRIATHLON

While most I. H. students are sleeping, eating breakfast, or trying to do the homework they should have done the night before, one student is hard at work, training for an athletic competition that would make Lisa Leslie weak in the knees.

Sophomore Ana Suarez is training for the upcoming triathlon in Central Park. Many people can run 6 kilometers, or swim 1.5 kilometers, or cycle 40 kilometers, but how many people can run, swim, and bike those distances in one day? Ms. Suarez can, and she says it is all because of her intensive training. "I've always loved sports, so the long hours of practice are fun hours."

Coach Kirov and Coach Arlen agree that Ana Suarez is a very talented athlete whose dedication and hard work will definitely pay off. Good luck in the triathlon, Ana!

SPORTS ARTICLES

Although sports articles are not "hard" news, they are a very important part of any school newspaper. First, many people turn directly to the sports section, so you are reaching a very large audience. Second, sports are an important part of school life: They serve to bring people together, encourage cooperation, and raise school spirit. For all of these reasons, the sports section is key to any school newspaper.

To write a news article:

Keep the following thoughts in mind when you are preparing to write a sports article:

• As with any other reporting, the key to writing a good sports article is preparation. You may be the best writer in your school, but if you don't know an end zone from a forward pass, your article about the football game won't make any sense. Speak to someone who is knowledgeable about the sport before you attend the event, read sports articles in other newspapers, and watch the sports on news shows to learn about the event you will be attending.

• If you are writing about a game or an event, try to speak to several of the athletes. Most sports stories include quotes from the players. This gives the article a more interesting tone.

• Sports have seasons, a period of time during which games are played. As the end of the season approaches, only those teams that have won most of their games will continue to play. These end-of-season games can be very exciting, especially if your team is playing!

• When you are covering a sporting event, take notes on which players performed well, which players did not, and also note the score at various points of the game. Sporting events can often be quite dramatic, with one team coming from behind in the last moments of the game to win. Try to pass this excitement on to your readers by keeping them in suspense as they read the article.

HAVE FUN!
ALWAYS REMEMBER WHAT
MR. TOUSSAINT SAYS:

WRITING=HONESTY=TRUTH

GENERATI✳N GIRL ™

available from Gold Key® paperbacks: